Disney
Vampirina

VEE'S MONSTER BASH

ADAPTED BY **CHELSEA BEYL**
BASED ON THE EPISODE "HAUNTLEYWEEN," WRITTEN BY **TRAVIS BRAUN**
ILLUSTRATED BY **IMAGINISM STUDIO**
AND THE **DISNEY STORYBOOK ART TEAM**

Disney PRESS
Los Angeles • New York

Copyright © 2018 Disney Enterprises, Inc. All rights reserved. Published by Disney Press, an imprint of Disney Book Group. No part of this book may be reproduced or transmitted in any form or by any means, electronic or mechanical, including photocopying, recording, or by any information storage and retrieval system, without written permission from the publisher. For information address Disney Press, 1200 Grand Central Avenue, Glendale, California 91201.

First Paperback Edition, July 2018   10 9 8 7 6 5 4 3 2 1

ISBN 978-1-368-02060-2

FAC-060025-18138

Library of Congress Control Number: 2017945889
Manufactured in China

For more Disney Press fun, visit www.disneybooks.com

SUSTAINABLE FORESTRY INITIATIVE
Certified Chain of Custody
Promoting Sustainable Forestry
www.sfiprogram.org
SFI-01415

"**M**AMA! PAPA! WAKE UP! WAKE UP!" Vampirina shouts, jumping on her parents' coffin.

Demi zooms in, too. "Yeah, wake up! Wake up!"

Vee is excited, because it's the day of her costume party.

"Is something going on today, Vee?" Oxana asks innocently.

Vee can't believe her parents forgot about the party! They sent out invitations to all their Transylvanian friends weeks ago. Vee reminds them that her human friends Poppy and Bridget are coming to the party, too.

"Well then, I guess it's a good thing Mama and I stayed up all night decorating," says Boris with a smile.

Vee zooms out of the room with Demi and Gregoria close behind.

When Vee gets downstairs, she's amazed! Spooky fog fills the living room, creepy spiders float through the air, cauldrons bubble over with green potions, and enchanted brooms dance around the house.

"It's spooktacular!" Vee exclaims. "I can't wait for my friends to see it! This is going to be the best costume party ever!"

Suddenly, Vee stops and thinks. Now that they live in Pennsylvania, what if their human neighbors spot their Transylvanian monster friends and get spooked?

"Don't worry," Demi says. "The humans will probably think the monsters are just humans *dressed up* as monsters for your costume party!"

Vee hopes Demi is right.

Vee hangs some decorations of her own before the party starts.
"Nothing says 'party' like extra-creepy cobwebs," she declares.
"Great job, batcakes!" says Oxana.

EEEEEK!

The Hauntleys' doorbell screams. Their first guests have arrived!
Vee opens the door.

"*AHHH!* Cowgirl! Giant cat!" Demi shrieks.

Vee explains that it's just Poppy and Bridget in their costumes.

"Where's *your* costume, Vee?" Poppy asks.

Vee shrugs. "We're kind of in ours year-round," she says, "being vampires and all."

Vee's doorbell shrieks again. "Our monster guests must be here!" she says.

Soon the Hauntleys' house is full of ghouls. There are mummies, goblins, witches, and even Vee's favorite band from Transylvania, the SCREAM GIRLS!

"You came all the way here for my party?" Vee squeals.

"We wouldn't miss it!" Franken-Stacey says.

EEEEEK!

The doorbell shrieks again. Vee opens the door, expecting more monster guests. But instead, she finds the Hauntleys' neighbors, Edna, Edgar, and Ms. Meyer.

"We heard about your little costume party and thought it would be fun to drop in," says Edna.

Vee panics. The entire house is full of spooky enchanted decorations!
"I think having a monster party in Pennsylvania was a bad
idea," she tells her parents. "We have to hide everything!"

Boris hides the hovering HEADSTONES. . . .

Oxana covers the bubbling
CAULDRONS. . . .

And Vee corners the conga-dancing
BROOMSTICKS!

Just then, Vee sees Edna and Ms. Meyer mingling with the monster guests. Edgar is even dancing with a little witch. "Cool costume," he says to the witch.

"They must think all the monsters are just humans wearing costumes," Vee says to her mom and dad, relieved.

DJ Demi grabs a mic. "Okay, all you monsters out there, it's time to put your tentacles, paws, and claws in the air like you just don't care!"

Humans and monsters boogie together like old friends.

But then Vee spots her pet werewolf, Wolfie!
"Oh, no! Wolfie's going to scare Edgar!" she says.
Before she can stop him, Wolfie bounds over to
Edgar and gives him a big slobbery lick.

Instead of being scared, Edgar just smiles. "Someone else came as a werewolf? Cool! We can be a pack!" he declares.

Then Edgar and Wolfie actually howl together.

"AWOOOOOOo!"

EEEEEK!

It's Vampirina's doorbell again. This time, it's Dr. Paquette, the critternarian from Transylvania. Vee is relieved it's not another human.

"I hope you don't mind, but I brought Brocknar, too!" says Dr. P.

"Brocknar?" Vampirina asks, craning her neck to look up at Brocknar, who happens to be an enormous dragon.

"Oh, no! There's no way any of the humans will think *that* is a costume!"
Vee says, worried. "We can't let everybody see a real fire-breathing dragon!"
Vee and her friends have to hide Brocknar . . . but where?

They try to hide Brocknar in the attic, but he's too squished.

They hide Brocknar in Vee's bedroom, but the dust makes him sneeze!

Just then, Vee has an idea. She grabs a remote control from her room and sticks an antenna to Brocknar's head. Then they sneak him out to the backyard.

When guests walk outside, Poppy is sitting on Brocknar's back.

"Who's up for a ride on my remote-control dragon?" shouts Vee, hoping no one will be scared away.

The humans have no idea Brocknar is real, and everybody loves him!
"You sure know how to throw a great MONSTER BASH!" says Poppy.
"Thanks!" says Vee. "Humans and monsters may
be different, but everyone likes to have fun!"